A Note from Michelle about
MY ALMOST PERFECT PLAN

Hi! I'm Michelle Tanner. I'm nine years old. And I just got picked to be on the all-star soccer team!

There's only one problem. My dad says I have to quit the team if I don't keep my grades up. But I don't have time for all my soccer practices *and* all my school work.

Or I didn't—until I figured out I could do my homework in the middle of the night. I just have to be careful not to wake anybody up. And that's hard, because my house is full of people.

There's my dad and my two older sisters, D.J. and Stephanie. But that's not all.

My mom died when I was little. So my uncle Jesse moved in to help Dad take care of us. So did Joey Gladstone. He's my dad's friend from college. It's almost like having three dads. But that's still not all!

First Uncle Jesse got married to Becky Donaldson. Then they had twin boys, Nicky and Alex. The twins are four years old now. And they're so cute.

That's nine people. Our dog, Comet, makes ten. Sure, it gets kind of crazy sometimes. But I wouldn't change it for anything. I love living in a full house!

FULL HOUSE™ MICHELLE novels

The Great Pet Project
The Super-Duper Sleepover Party
My Two Best Friends
Lucky, Lucky Day
The Ghost in My Closet
Ballet Surprise
Major League Trouble
My Fourth-Grade Mess
Bunk 3, Teddy and Me
My Best Friend Is a Movie Star! (Super Special)
The Big Turkey Escape
The Substitute Teacher
Calling All Planets
I've Got a Secret
How to Be Cool
The Not-So-Great Outdoors
My Ho-Ho-Horrible Christmas
My Almost Perfect Plan

Activity Book
My Awesome Holiday Friendship Book

Available from MINSTREL Books

FULL HOUSE™
Michelle

My Almost Perfect Plan

Sarah J. Verney

A Parachute Book

Published by POCKET BOOKS

New York London Toronto Sydney Tokyo Singapore

A MINSTREL PAPERBACK *Original*

A Minstrel Book published by
POCKET BOOKS, a division of Simon & Schuster Inc.
1230 Avenue of the Americas, New York, NY 10020

A PARACHUTE PRESS BOOK

READING Copyright © and ™ 1998 by Warner Bros.

ISBN: 0-671-00837-4

First Minstrel Books printing February 1998

10 9 8 7 6 5 4 3 2 1

Cover photo by Schultz Photography

Printed in the U.S.A.

Chapter
1

♥ "Wow! I still can't believe they picked me!" Michelle Tanner cried. "Thanks so, so much for calling."

Michelle hung up the phone and punched a fist in the air. "Yes!" she said, and ran into the kitchen. She had to tell somebody her amazing news.

"Guess what," Michelle shouted.

"What?" Michelle's father, Danny Tanner, asked. He stood at the kitchen counter, tearing up lettuce for a salad.

"I'm going to be—" Michelle began.

Comet, the Tanner's golden retriever, raced into the room. Nicky and Alex, Michelle's four-year-old twin cousins, dashed into the room after the big dog.

"Michelle, come play space aliens with us," Nicky begged.

Michelle shook her head. "I can't right now. I have something important to tell Dad."

"Maybe Stephanie will play with us," Alex said. "Come on!" He raced out of the kitchen with Comet and Nicky right behind him.

Michelle was sure the twins would find someone to play with them. That was one good thing about being in a big family. There were always tons of people to play with at any time.

Besides Michelle, her dad, and thirteen-year-old Stephanie, there was D.J., Michelle's eighteen-year-old sister. She was in college.

Then there were Uncle Jesse and Aunt

Becky, Alex and Nicky's parents. Uncle Jesse moved in a long time ago, when Michelle's mother died. Michelle was just a baby then. Later he and Aunt Becky got married, and she moved in too.

Joey Gladstone, her dad's best friend, also moved in when Michelle's mom died. That made nine people in Michelle's family.

Michelle loved living in such a full house. Especially when she had something exciting to share. Like now.

"Hey, Dad," Michelle started again. "I've got really good news."

Joey walked in while she was talking and scooped Michelle into a big hug. "You're getting married! Oh, Michelle, I'm so happy for you!" He squished her face against his bright orange and pink Hawaiian shirt.

"Jo-ey!" Michelle giggled and pulled away. Joey was always kidding around. "No way!"

Michelle was nine years old. She didn't plan on getting married anytime soon.

"Don't you even want to know what my great news—" Michelle began.

The back door banged open. D.J. raced in, waving a piece of paper. "Look! An A plus on my English paper!"

"That's great! And you know what other great thing happened today?" Michelle asked.

Aunt Becky and Uncle Jesse burst into the kitchen with the twins. "We want dinner!" Nicky exclaimed. "Nobody wants to play space aliens."

"Perfect timing," Michelle's dad said. "It's ready. Everyone go sit at the table."

Michelle hurried over to the big table and sat down. Stephanie strolled in and took her place across from Michelle.

Okay, Michelle thought. Everybody's here. This is the perfect time to tell my big news. Michelle took a deep breath and opened her mouth.

"Boy, I've got to get back in shape," her dad complained before Michelle could say a word. "I am so stiff, just from rearranging some furniture. I can't stand it!"

"Why don't you join a gym?" Becky suggested.

"And go when? I'm always busy with the TV show or the house. I don't have enough time," Danny said.

Michelle jumped up from the table. She couldn't wait one more second. "Doesn't anyone want to hear my super-fantastic good news?" she demanded.

"I'm sorry, honey. You keep getting interrupted, don't you?" her dad answered. "Go ahead. We're all listening."

"Go on, tell us, Michelle," D.J. said.

"Yeah, tell us," Stephanie added.

Michelle glanced around the table. No one was eating. Everyone was waiting to hear her announcement. Finally.

"I made the all-star soccer team! The Dolphins," she told them. "The coach called and told me a little while ago."

"I thought soccer was over for the year," D.J. said.

"No, the all-star season starts after the regular season," Michelle explained. She bounced up and down on her toes. She still could hardly believe it was true. She could hardly believe she was an all-star.

Everyone congratulated Michelle at once.

"I'm really proud of you, Michelle," Danny said. "You worked hard this season."

"Only one or two girls from each team get chosen," Michelle explained. "I was the one from my team! Isn't that great?"

"We'll all have to go out and celebrate," Danny said. "It's the first time we've had an all-star in the family."

Michelle sat back down. "First there are a few games to decide the top teams. Then they get to be in the playoffs," she told them.

"I think it's wonderful that you made the team," Danny said. "All those games are going to take a lot of time. And you're already busy. You have art classes and piano lessons. And you need to start spending more time on your schoolwork. Remember that C you got on your last history test?"

"I know, I know," Michelle said. "I'll do better, I promise."

"I'm just not sure you have the time," her dad said. "Maybe you should tell the coach that you can't be on the all-star team this year."

No way! Michelle thought. He can't really mean it.

Chapter

2

♥ "But I have to be on the team, Dad," Michelle cried.

"I know it's important to you," Danny said. "But you got a C on your last book report too. Remember?"

Michelle frowned. Her dad was right. She had gotten a couple of C's. But she could do better. She knew it.

"I'll study harder. I promise." Michelle stared at her dad. Please say yes, she thought. Please, please, please.

"I'm sorry. I just don't think it's a good

idea. You'll have another chance next year," Danny said.

Michelle stabbed a noodle with her fork. It wasn't fair! She might not even get chosen for the all-stars next year. Tears stung her eyes.

"What if Michelle promises to put her schoolwork first?" Aunt Becky asked. "If she gets anything lower than a B on her next report card, you could take her off the team."

Michelle crossed all of her fingers on both hands.

"But it wouldn't be fair to the other players if she had to quit in the middle of the tournament," Danny said.

"That won't happen," Michelle promised. "I'll work really hard. I know I can do it. Really. Please."

Danny stared down at his plate of spaghetti and frowned. Michelle tried to cross her toes.

"All right," Danny said at last. "But those

grades have to come up. Nothing lower than a B, Michelle. And no excuses."

"Yes!" Michelle jumped out of her chair and ran to hug her father. "Thanks, Dad."

Danny put an arm around her waist and gave a little squeeze. "Just remember, Michelle. No excuses."

"All right, girls, everybody grab a partner," Coach Oliver called. He ran a hand through his sandy-blond hair.

Michelle looked around. It was her very first team practice, and she didn't recognize many of the other kids. She smiled at a red-haired girl standing next to her. "Hi. You want to be partners?" she asked. "I'm Michelle."

"Sure," the girl said. "I'm Jenny. You ever been on an all-star team before?" She tossed a soccer ball up and caught it.

"No," Michelle said. "Have you?"

"Yeah. Last year my team made it all the way to the semifinals," Jenny told her.

"Wow. That's so cool," Michelle said.

"This year I think we could make it to the finals." Jenny looked around. "A lot of these girls are really good. What grade are you in?" she asked Michelle.

"Fourth," Michelle answered.

"Only fourth? Really?" Jenny asked. "I'm in fifth. I think most of these girls are older than you." Jenny set the ball on the ground and popped it up with her toe. She caught it.

Michelle studied the other girls. Almost everyone was bigger than she was. She stood up straight to look as tall as possible. I'm as good as they are, she told herself. I wouldn't have been picked for the team if I wasn't.

Phweet! Coach Oliver blew his whistle. "All right, girls! I want each set of partners to run down the field, passing the ball back and forth. Everybody ready? Go."

Jenny ran a few feet and passed the ball to Michelle. Michelle kicked it back. The ball zoomed past Jenny.

Oops! Jenny had to run after the ball to get it.

Jenny passed the ball back to Michelle. Don't kick it so hard this time, Michelle told herself. She wanted the ball to go right to Jenny—not past her.

Michelle gave the ball a light kick. It didn't even make it halfway to Jenny.

Two of the other girls ran past Michelle and Jenny. They passed the ball back and forth with no problems. They're really good, Michelle thought.

Another pair of girls raced past. They both had perfect control of the ball too.

"Don't make me run for it," Jenny yelled. "You've got to kick it straight to me." She booted the ball back to Michelle.

Michelle kicked the ball. Oh, no! It landed *behind* Jenny. "Sorry."

Jenny shook her head. She kicked the ball right back to Michelle.

Two more girls ran by them. The ball whizzed back and forth between them.

Michelle glanced around at the rest of her teammates. Everyone is watching us, she realized. We're the last ones. She felt her face turn red.

"All right," Coach Oliver called when Michelle and Jenny finally made it to the end of the field. "Good job. But some of you could use a little extra practice at home on this one." The coach stared right at Michelle.

Michelle looked down at her sneakers.

"Now let's work on stealing the ball," Coach Oliver said. "One girl will dribble the ball. The other will try to take it away. Go!"

Jenny took off down the field with the ball. Michelle chased after her. Jenny moved so fast! How was Michelle going to get the ball away from her?

You can do it, Michelle told herself. Ready . . . one, two, three, *go!* Michelle lunged toward the ball. Her feet tangled up with Jenny's.

Boom! Michelle landed on the ground.

Michelle shook her head as she watched Jenny race down the field with the ball. Maybe Michelle had been the best player on her old soccer team. But now she was the worst on her new team!

Chapter

3

♥ Michelle pointed to Stephanie's initials on the chart. "See, Steph, you're signed up for four-thirty on Thursday. That's today, in one hour, in the backyard. Be there!"

After her first soccer practice, Michelle knew she needed help. A lot of help.

She signed up everyone in the family to practice soccer with her. She figured it was the only way to get good enough to keep up with the rest of her team.

The extra practices were helping a little. But she needed a lot more work.

"Michelle," Stephanie groaned. "I've got stuff to do. I've practically worn out a pair of sneakers running around the backyard with you."

"Stephanie, you promised. What's more important, that stuff, or the soccer tournament?" Michelle asked.

"Now that you asked—" Stephanie began.

"You want me to be good, don't you?" Michelle interrupted.

"Well . . ." Stephanie hesitated.

"I really need help, Steph! You don't want me to embarrass the Tanner family, do you? I've got to get better. Puh-leeze. Pretty please with chocolate cheesecake on top?" Michelle begged.

"Oh, okay," Stephanie said. "Four-thirty in the backyard."

"Thanks!" Michelle smiled and ran out of their room. She almost smacked into Danny on the stairs. He was on his way up, carrying a vacuum cleaner.

"Dad!" Michelle exclaimed. "What are you doing? It's your turn!"

"Huh? Already? I did soccer drills with you three days ago," Danny answered.

"Joey and Uncle Jesse helped the day before yesterday," Michelle said. Aunt Becky and D.J. helped yesterday. Today it's you and Stephanie."

Danny looked at the vacuum cleaner. "Well, I guess I can do this later. But don't you have homework?"

"A little," Michelle said. She had a book report due the next day. "But I can do it later, after it's too dark to practice." She took his hand and pulled him down the stairs.

"Are you sure you'll have enough time, Michelle? Remember your promise," Danny warned. "Your grades get better. No excuses."

"I know, Dad, I know," Michelle said. "Don't worry!"

Michelle pulled Danny out into the backyard. She grabbed the soccer ball and started dribbling across the lawn. "You try to take it away from me!" Michelle called.

Michelle and Danny raced back and forth. Michelle could hear her dad huffing and puffing as he ran.

"Stop!" Danny cried after four trips up and down the lawn. "Hold on." He leaned over, breathing hard.

"Gee, Dad, you really are out of shape," Michelle commented.

Danny wiped a trickle of sweat off his forehead. "I know," he said. "I should go to a gym. But there's never enough time."

"Well, come on, then," Michelle said. "Let's try passing now. That'll get you in shape." She kicked the ball toward Danny.

"Okay, coach, whatever you say," Danny answered.

Michelle put her book down on the bed. "Hey, Stephanie! Have you got any socks with green stripes?"

"Green stripes! Why?" Stephanie looked up from her desk. She was doing her homework in the room she and Michelle shared.

"Because I was reading about this famous soccer player, José Pepa. He always wears green-striped socks for good luck," Michelle explained.

"So?" Stephanie pushed her blond hair behind her ears.

"So if they bring him good luck, maybe they could work for me too," Michelle explained. "I wonder if Dad could make black beans and rice before my games. The book says José always eats them. They give him lots of energy."

"Yeah, and lots of gas too." Stephanie laughed. "That'll make you real popular with your teammates."

"Stephanie, this is serious," Michelle protested. She stood and picked up Moochie, an old teddy bear of Stephanie's. "I have to get better at soccer. I just have to."

"Uh-huh," Stephanie said. She went back to her homework.

Michelle sighed. She ran her fingers over Moochie's fur. Maybe she'd try something she read about in a book. She was supposed to picture herself doing something really great in her sport. The book said that would help to do it in real life.

Michelle closed her eyes and pictured herself running down the soccer field. She dribbled the ball perfectly. Other players tried to steal it, but she was too quick.

Michelle saw the goal in front of her. She gave the ball a hard, solid kick. It sailed right past the goalie. Yes!

"Michelle! What do you think you're doing!"

"Huh?" Michelle opened her eyes.

Stephanie glared at her. "You kicked Moochie!"

Michelle spotted the teddy bear halfway across the room. Uh-oh! "Sorry," she told Stephanie. She hurried over to the teddy bear and picked him up. "I guess I got carried away."

"Hmmph." Stephanie took the bear and patted him on the head. "Poor old Moochiemoo," she murmured.

Michelle rolled her eyes. She picked up her book and climbed into bed. It was almost time to turn out the light. But she could read her book for a little—

Her book! Michelle sat up suddenly. Oh, no! She'd forgotten her book report.

Michelle groaned. What was she going to do?

"What's the matter?" Stephanie asked.

"Uh, nothing," Michelle said quickly. She didn't want to admit she'd messed up. Stephanie knew Michelle had promised to get better grades.

Michelle gulped. She was dead. How was she supposed to get a good report card if she didn't even turn her homework in?

Michelle looked at the clock. In five minutes her dad would be up to turn off the light and say good night. She was running out of time.

I wish I could stay up as late as D.J., Michelle thought. Then I would have plenty of time to get my book report done.

Sometimes D.J. didn't go to bed until midnight when she had a big paper to do for one of her college classes.

Maybe if she told her dad she'd forgotten a teensy bit of her homework, he'd let her stay up and finish.

No. Michelle knew exactly what he'd say. "No, excuses, Michelle. Remember?"

It was so frustrating. There were hours, and hours, and hours before school tomorrow. More than enough hours to finish her book report. But she couldn't use them, because she had to be in bed.

Or maybe not, Michelle thought. Maybe there was a way. . . .

Chapter
4

♥ *Brriiinnng.*

Why doesn't somebody answer the phone? Michelle thought.

Brriiinnng.

Michelle sat straight up in bed. Because it's not the phone—it's my alarm clock!

Michelle reached under her pillow, where she had hidden the clock to quiet the sound. She didn't want to wake Stephanie up.

She turned off the alarm. One A.M. She'd never been up that late before.

It is the perfect time to do my book report, though, Michelle thought. The house is so quiet.

Michelle slid slowly out of bed, careful not to make any noise. She didn't want to wake up Stephanie. Or anybody else.

She tiptoed to the closet and got her slippers. Then she picked up her book, some paper, and a pencil from her desk.

Michelle silently opened the door and slipped out into the hall. So far, so good, she thought as she crept along the dark hallway. She slowly headed down the stairs, careful to avoid the creaky step near the bottom.

Then she scurried through the living room and into the kitchen. She made it without waking anybody up. Yay!

Michelle flipped on the overhead light and sat down at the table. She carefully wrote her name, the title of the book, and the author's name at the top of a piece of paper.

Now what? She gave a big yawn. She couldn't think of one thing to write for her book report.

It's hard to think this late at night. It's like my brain knows it should be asleep, Michelle thought.

She flipped through the book. She just finished reading it yesterday, but she was having trouble remembering the plot.

Maybe if I put my head down for a minute it will help. I'll just take a five-minute nap, Michelle told herself.

No! She shook her head. She had to stay awake.

Maybe I should put the TV on, Michelle thought. Her dad didn't usually let her do her homework in front of the TV, but she needed *something* to keep her from falling asleep.

Besides, her dad didn't let her do homework in the middle of the night either. So what did it matter?

Michelle took her book and her paper and headed back into the living room. It's so quiet, she thought. She could hear the clock over the mantel ticking.

She clicked through the channels until she found a show called *How to Do Everything Better.* A lady was talking about how to get water marks off wood tables with toothpaste.

Dad would love this show, Michelle thought. I have to remember some of this stuff for him.

When a commercial came on, Michelle switched to a cooking show. A man in a tall white hat chopped onions and told silly jokes. It wasn't the best show Michelle had ever seen. But she watched for a while anyway.

She flipped to another channel. Two women were modeling clothes. Another person talked about what they were wearing.

It was fun having complete control over the remote. That didn't happen very often in her house. Too many people.

Michelle glanced at the clock on the mantel. Yikes! It was two o'clock! She'd been up an hour already, and she had written hardly anything. Maybe having the TV on wasn't such a good idea after all.

She flicked off the TV. Then she stood up and gave a big stretch.

I need a snack before I start work again, Michelle decided. She wandered into the kitchen. She made a peanut butter and raisin sandwich and a big glass of chocolate milk. Then she sat down at the table.

Okay, first I should tell what the story is about, Michelle thought. She started to write and filled up half the page.

Now I should explain what I liked or didn't like. That's what her teacher, Mrs. Yoshida, said to do. Michelle nibbled on the side of her pencil, then started to write again.

Creak! What was that? Michelle thought.

I know! It was the step near the bottom of the stairs. It always creaks when someone steps on it.

She sat absolutely still and listened.

Voices! Someone was coming toward the kitchen!

Michelle jumped up and turned off the light. She folded her paper and shoved it into the book. But where could she go? Not back out to the living room. That was where the voices were.

The voices were louder now. Michelle's heart started to pound. She ducked under the kitchen table. Maybe they wouldn't see her.

Oh, no! She forgot her plate and glass. Michelle popped out from under the table and grabbed them. Then she dove back into her hiding place.

The door to the kitchen opened and someone turned on the light. Michelle peered out from under the table. It was Uncle Jesse and Nicky. "Your cough medicine must be in here, Nicky," Jesse said. "I don't know where else we could have left it."

Michelle held her breath as Jesse led

Nicky over to the sink. Nicky turned around—and looked right at her.

Nicky started to point at Michelle. Then he coughed. He covered his mouth with both hands.

"Here it is," Jesse said. "This will fix you up, buddy. Let's go back upstairs and I'll give you some."

Nicky stopped coughing. "Michelle," he yelled. "Michelle, Michelle."

Oh, no!

She was caught!

Chapter
5

♥ "No, Nicky, Michelle is sleeping right now," Jesse said. "She can't play." He pulled Nicky out of the kitchen, flipping off the light as he went.

Michelle let her breath out in a *whoosh*. Wow, that was close, she thought. She crawled out from under the table and waited, listening. She didn't hear a sound.

She was safe, and her book report was almost done! Staying up all night was all right.

* * *

"Michelle! Stephanie! D.J! Dinner!"

Michelle jumped up from the couch. How could it be dinnertime? She just got home from her soccer game.

"Come on, Michelle." Stephanie took her hand and pulled her into the dining room. "What's wrong with you?"

Michelle shook her head. "I guess I fell asleep."

Maybe I should cut back on my late-night homework sessions, she thought. Michelle had gotten up in the middle of the night four more nights since she wrote her book report.

She got a lot done. But she was getting really tired. She fell asleep while Mrs. Yoshida was reading to them that afternoon. Mandy told her she even started to snore a little.

It was so embarrassing. Plus she missed the best part of the story.

I shouldn't have eaten turkey for lunch, Michelle thought. The man on the TV show *How to Do Everything Better* said there was something in turkey that may make you sleepy. And Michelle didn't need to be any sleepier.

"You must be worn out from your game," her dad commented when Michelle sat down at the table.

"How did it go?" Aunt Becky asked.

"It was awful," Michelle answered. "I really blew it. The score was tied, and Jenny passed the ball to me. I was right in front of the goal."

Michelle stared down at her plate. She mixed her green beans into her mashed potatoes.

"So what happened?" Stephanie asked.

"It was my big chance," Michelle said. "One kick would get us a goal—and win us the game. I pulled my foot back as far as I could. I wanted to kick the ball *hard.*"

Michelle groaned. "But I missed it. My shoe didn't even touch the ball. A girl from the other team stole the ball and made a goal for *her* side. So the Dolphins lost."

"You have another game on the weekend," Danny reminded her. "You'll have lots more chances to make a goal."

"You're right!" Michelle cried. "But I need more practice. If I get up an hour earlier, I can do some drills before school." Michelle stared around the table. "Any volunteers to help me?"

D.J. sighed. "Put me down for Tuesday morning."

"I'll take Wednesday," Joey said.

In seconds Michelle had a practice buddy for every morning of the week.

"Just don't forget to schedule time for your schoolwork," Danny said.

Schoolwork. That was what she should have been doing before dinner. She had a big social studies test on Friday, and she hadn't even started studying. If she wanted to get a B in social studies on her report card, she had to get at least a B on that test.

I'll start studying right after dinner, she thought.

The second she had swallowed the last bite of her meat loaf, she asked to be excused. Then she hurried into the living room and grabbed her social studies book.

She read the first two paragraphs—and then the doorbell rang.

Michelle ran over and opened the door. Her best friend, Cassie Wilkins, stood on the front porch.

"What are you doing here?" Michelle exclaimed. Then she remembered. "Oh, yeah! The mall. Mandy's birthday present." She hit her forehead with her hand.

Mandy Metz was Michelle's other best friend. Her birthday was this weekend, and Cassie and Michelle needed to buy her a present.

"Wait right here," Michelle told her friend. She raced into the dining room. "Dad, Cassie's here. Her mom's taking us to the mall to get Mandy's birthday present. I forgot all about it. Can I go? We won't take long. I promise I'll be home early."

And I promise I'll study for my test as soon as I get back, Michelle added to herself.

"Look," Cassie said. "There are the twins. And Amber too."

Michelle followed Cassie's gaze and saw the twins, Debbie and Donna, and Amber. They all went to Michelle's school.

"Let's go say hi," Michelle suggested. They hurried over.

"What did you get?" Cassie asked Amber. She pointed to the little bag Amber held in one hand.

"Just a barrette," Amber said. "I wanted one to match my new sweater."

"I know a hairstyle that would look really cool on you," Michelle told her.

She pulled back a section of hair from each side of Amber's face. "See? You put rubber bands in both of these, and then"— Michelle twisted them together the way the lady had on TV—"and then you put the barrette here."

"Wow!" Amber said. "That's so easy. Thanks Michelle."

"My hair's long enough to do that too," Debbie said. She frowned. "Except I can't pull it back, because look at this."

She held out a piece of hair. "Can you believe it? My little sister got gum in my hair after school today. I just keep tucking this piece behind my ear, so you can't see it."

"Peanut butter!" Michelle cried. "If you put peanut butter in your hair, it will make it all slippery and the gum will slide out."

"That's so cool!" Debbie cried. "I'll try it. Thanks."

Cassie nudged Michelle with her elbow. "Hey, we'd better go," she said. "Or we won't have enough time to find a present."

"You're right," Michelle said. "I promised my dad I'd get home early. She waved to her friends. "Bye, everybody."

"How do you know all that stuff?" Cassie asked as they hurried off to join Cassie's mom.

"I saw it on a TV show," Michelle answered. She didn't tell Cassie the show was on in the middle of the night. That was Michelle's little secret.

Brriiinnng.

How could the alarm be ringing already? Michelle felt as if she had been asleep for only a few minutes.

Michelle snapped off the alarm. She lay still and listened. The house was silent.

Good. The alarm didn't wake anyone, Michelle thought.

She tiptoed downstairs to the living room. Then she crept over to the sofa, where she had left her social studies book. She had to be quiet, quiet, quiet if she didn't want to get caught.

She got home from the mall so late, she

37

didn't have time to study for her big test on Friday. She had to do it now.

Michelle spied her soccer ball near the coffee table. But I need to practice too, she thought. She snagged the ball with her toe and dribbled toward the kitchen.

Okay, she thought. I'll pretend the doorway is the goal. It's time to score some points! She gave the ball a hard kick.

It sailed up, up, up . . .

Then down—right on top of a lamp.

Crash!

Chapter
6

♥ Michelle heard Danny's bedroom door open.

She heard Joey pounding up the stairs from the basement.

Yikes! She was in big trouble now. If her dad found out she was getting up in the middle of the night to do homework, she would have to quit the all-stars for sure.

Michelle threw her social studies book behind a couch cushion. Then she rubbed her eyes and tried to look really sleepy.

Danny ran down the stairs. Joey burst into the living room.

"Michelle? What happened?" her dad exclaimed.

Michelle rubbed her eyes again. "I don't know," she said, pretending to be confused. "What's going on? How did I get here?"

"You mean you don't know?" Joey asked.

"Unh-unh." Michelle widened her eyes in surprise. "Who knocked over the lamp?"

This better work, she thought.

"You must have," Joey said. "You were the only one here."

"Oh." Michelle said. She rubbed her eyes and yawned again. "I don't remember anything. I thought I was in bed." She peeked up at her dad. Did he believe her?

Michelle saw her dad exchange a glance with Joey. "Sleepwalking?" Danny asked Joey.

Joey shrugged. "I guess," he said.

"That's funny," Danny said. "She's never done it before."

"There's a first time for everything," Joey said.

Michelle's heart pounded so hard, she thought Danny and Joey would hear it. Are they going to believe me? she wondered.

Danny shook his head. "Weird," he said. "Come on, Michelle. How about I take you back to your bed?"

"Okay," she said. She let her dad put an arm around her shoulder and lead her up-stairs.

Michelle climbed back into her bed. Danny leaned over and kissed her on the forehead. "I wish I could walk in my sleep. I might get a little exercise that way," he joked. "Good night, Michelle."

"Good night, Daddy." Michelle closed her eyes.

Oh, well, she thought. So I won't study for my test tonight. There's always tomorrow.

Coach Oliver blew his whistle. "Listen up, Dolphins," he said. "We're down by one goal, but let's not get discouraged. I know we can beat the Scorpions if we work together! Now, let's get out there!"

Michelle's heart pounded as she ran out onto the field. Be like José, she told herself. Get a goal!

She had spent the first half of the game on the bench. But now she would have the chance to show everyone she deserved to be an all-star.

The whistle blew. Michelle ran down the field. Two girls fought for control of the ball. One of them knocked it toward Michelle.

She snagged it and took off dribbling down the field. All right!

Two players from the Scorpion team moved in. Michelle searched the field. Who could she pass to?

"Here, Michelle!" Jenny yelled.

Michelle tapped the ball with the side of her foot, and it sailed straight to Jenny.

"Way to go, Michelle!" Coach Oliver

shouted. Michelle grinned. All that practice has paid off, she thought.

Jenny drove the ball down the field. Two Scorpions closed in on her. They scrambled to get the ball—and it flew into the air.

Michelle raced up and stopped the ball with her shoulder. It dropped to her feet. Michelle didn't stop to think. She pounded the field as fast as she could go.

She passed the ball to a girl named Angela, and Angela slammed it into the goal! They scored!

"Yes!" Michelle screamed. She punched a fist in the air as she ran back to center field with her teammates.

Michelle couldn't stop smiling the rest of the game. She smiled when she stole the ball from the Scorpions. She smiled when she passed the ball to the other girls on her team. She smiled when her team scored, and she smiled extra big when they won the game!

"Hey, Michelle," Angela called to her as

they gathered around Coach Oliver after the game. "You were great! You're getting really good at stealing the ball."

"Thanks." Michelle bounced up and down on her toes. She felt so happy, she couldn't stand still.

"Yeah," Jenny said. "It's like she's our secret weapon."

"Who wants pizza and ice cream?" Coach Oliver asked. The girls all cheered.

"All right, then! Go ask your parents' permission!" He waved them away.

Michelle ran over to Danny.

"Great game, Michelle," he said. "You were fantastic. I wish I could run around the field as fast as you do."

"Thanks, Dad!" Michelle gave him a hug. Danny groaned.

"What's wrong?" Michelle cried.

"I think I hurt my back when I was taking out the garbage last night. I really have to start exercising more," he answered.

"Come on, Michelle," Jenny yelled.

"The coach is taking us out for pizza and ice cream," Michelle told Danny. "Can I go?"

"I think you deserve to celebrate," Danny said. "But what about your homework?"

"It's almost done," Michelle said. She *still* hadn't studied for the social studies test. But she was sure she could do that when she got home.

"Okay, Michelle. Just remember—"

"I know, I know," Michelle interrupted. "No excuses!"

"Michelle, wake up! It's time to get ready for school." Stephanie shook Michelle by the shoulder.

School? Michelle snapped her eyes open and stared around the room. Sunlight streamed in through the windows.

"It's morning already?" she asked.

"Sure," Stephanie said cheerfully. "It's almost time for breakfast. You'd better hurry." She grabbed her backpack.

"Oh, man!" Stephanie exclaimed. "I just got a run in my tights."

"You should put them in the freezer before you wear them," Michelle told her. At least that's what the man on *How to Do Everything Better* said.

"Really?" Stephanie shrugged. "I'll try it." She rushed out the door.

Michelle pulled the alarm clock out from under her pillow and checked it. She forgot to push the little button in—so the alarm hadn't gone off!

Her social studies test was this morning, and she never studied for it.

She was doomed.

Chapter

7

♥ Michelle stumbled out of bed and shuffled into the bathroom.

Maybe I should pretend to be sick, she thought. Then I could get a makeup test.

No, she had a soccer game after school. If she pretended to be sick, she wouldn't be able to play in the game.

Michelle picked up her toothbrush and squeezed on some toothpaste. What am I going to do? she thought.

She started to brush her teeth. Tons of bubbles foamed out of her mouth.

Yuck! The toothpaste tasted terrible.

That's because it's not toothpaste—it's shampoo! Michelle realized.

She grabbed her glass and filled it with water. She rinsed her mouth out again and again.

Michelle shook her head. I can't believe I put shampoo on my toothbrush, she thought. I must be more tired than I realized.

I hope I don't fall asleep during the test!

Michelle stared at the sheet of paper before her. "Social Studies Test, Unit 3," it said at the top. "Ancient Egypt." The questions below looked hard. Really hard.

"All right, everyone," Mrs. Yoshida said. "You know the rules. Keep your eyes on your own paper. When you're finished, turn the test over. You may now begin."

Michelle read through the test quickly. She hardly knew any of the answers! What was she going to do? If she messed up on this test, her father would make her quit the team for sure.

Michelle chewed on the tip of her pencil. She glanced around the room. Cassie was busy filling in answer after answer.

Social studies is Cassie's best subject, Michelle thought. I bet she's going to get an A.

If Michelle leaned over just an inch, she would be able to see Cassie's paper. Should she do it? Michelle had never copied before, but this was an emergency.

Michelle looked up at Mrs. Yoshida. She was writing their homework assignment on the chalkboard. She wouldn't catch Michelle if Michelle peeked at Cassie's paper.

Should I do it? Michelle wondered again.

Mrs. Yoshida glanced over her shoulder and her eyes met Michelle's. Michelle felt her cheeks get hot. She bent her head and stared down at her paper.

No! She couldn't do it. She *wouldn't*. She wasn't a cheater!

Michelle read through the test again. She

knew three answers. Three—out of twenty-five. She swallowed hard.

She slowly filled in the three answers. Then she read the test again. And again.

Michelle gripped her pencil tighter. She read the test one more time.

"Five more minutes," Mrs. Yoshida called.

Oh, no! I'll guess on the true-and-false ones, and the multiple choice, Michelle decided. Maybe I'll get *some* right.

Mrs. Yoshida walked to the front of the classroom. "You may exchange papers with your neighbor now," she said. "Please take out your red pencils."

Michelle and Cassie traded tests.

"Is everyone ready?" Mrs. Yoshida asked. "Okay, here we go. Number one—true."

I got that one wrong, Michelle thought.

"Number two—false."

That one too!

"Number three—false."

Michelle felt tears sting her eyes as Mrs.

Yoshida read off the rest of the answers. She really messed up.

"Sorry," Cassie said as she handed Michelle's paper back. Up at the top, Cassie had written the letter D in tiny print.

A D! Michelle had never gotten a D in her whole life. And this test was a big part of her social studies grade.

Report cards came out at the end of next week. She was never going to be able to bring her social studies grade up to a B before then.

Michelle folded down the top of her paper to hide the D. She didn't even want to look at it.

What was she going to do? She loved being on the all-star team. She couldn't quit now. The Dolphins still had a chance to make it to the playoffs. And she was the team's secret weapon!

But as soon as her dad saw her report card, she knew she would have to quit.

Chapter

8

♥ "I really blew it!" Michelle wailed. She slammed her tray down on the cafeteria table.

"Calm down, Michelle," Mandy said.

"Yeah," Cassie agreed. "It's only one grade. You'll do better on the next test."

Michelle slumped down in her seat. "Then it will be too late," she said. "Now I won't be able to get better than a C on my report card. My dad said if I got anything lower than a B, I would have to quit the all-star team."

"Maybe he'll change his mind," Mandy said.

Michelle shook her head. No excuses. That's what her dad kept telling her.

"Michelle!" Her friend Lucy Tibbons hurried up to their table. "I have to ask you something.

"What?" Michelle looked up, surprised. Laura Matthews and Mary Beth Alonzo, two other girls from Mrs. Yoshida's class, followed close behind Lucy.

"I love the way you taught Amber to do her hair," Lucy gushed. "You've got to show me how to do it."

"Not right now," she said. "Sorry." She was too upset to think about hairstyles.

Then Michelle remembered something a lady on TV had said about face shapes. "You shouldn't wear your hair pulled back anyway," she said.

"I shouldn't?"

"No." Michelle studied Lucy's round face and almond-shaped eyes. "You should cut some bangs," she said. "And part your hair on the side, not in the middle."

"Really?" Lucy said eagerly. "Okay, I'll try it."

"What about me?" Laura asked.

"Your haircut is exactly right for your face," Michelle answered. "But you should try putting rose hip tea in it. That's supposed to brighten up red hair."

"Thanks. I'm going to try it tonight," Aimee said.

"Don't forget about me," Mary Beth told Michelle.

Michelle started to feel a teeny, tiny bit better. It was cool having everyone ask her for advice.

She told everyone at the table what colors they would look best in. She told her friend Jeff how he could train his dog to wake him up in the morning. She told Cassie how to make gift wrap using her mom's computer. Then she gave Mandy a recipe for making

Play-Doh. Mandy's littlest brother loved Play-Doh.

"Boy, you know everything, Michelle," Mandy exclaimed.

Michelle grinned. Then she remembered the D on her test. "Mrs. Yoshida won't think I know *anything* when she sees my test."

"Hey, wait a minute," Cassie cried. "I just had an idea. Why don't you ask Mrs. Yoshida if you can do some extra-credit? Then you'll get a good enough grade to stay on the soccer team."

"That's a great idea!" Michelle said. "Come on!" She raced down the hall to the classroom, with Mandy and Cassie close behind her.

Michelle burst into the classroom. "Mrs. Yoshida!"

The teacher looked up from her desk. "Yes, Michelle?"

"I know that I didn't do very well on the test," Michelle said.

Mrs. Yoshida nodded, and Michelle

rushed on. "Could I do an extra-credit project, please? On the pyramids or something?"

"Well, I—"

"Please, Mrs. Yoshida," Michelle begged. "I know I should have studied harder. I really want to do something to bring my grade up."

Mrs. Yoshida smiled. "I think an extra-credit project is a terrific idea."

"Yes!" Michelle gave Cassie and Mandy high-fives. "Thank you, Mrs. Yoshida. Thank you, thank you, thank you!"

Mrs. Yoshida laughed. "One thank-you is plenty. There's just one condition," she told Michelle. "Your project has to be something that shows me what you've learned about ancient Egypt. What did you have in mind?"

Michelle thought fast. "How about a diorama?" she suggested. That would be fun and easy.

"Well . . ." Mrs. Yoshida hesitated. "How about a diorama with a little extra information on index cards," she said. "Facts about the pyramids and the Egyptians."

"Okay," Michelle agreed. "I'll do it. I'll do anything."

"Turn it in to me on Wednesday," Mrs. Yoshida said.

Wednesday! Michelle took a deep breath and blew it out slowly. She counted off the days she had to work. Five days—counting today.

That wasn't much time. She and Cassie were sleeping over at Mandy's tonight because it was Mandy's birthday. She had soccer practice on Saturday afternoon.

Then the whole family was going to see D.J. in a play at her college on Saturday night. Michelle couldn't miss that.

On Sunday she had a soccer game. She definitely couldn't miss that.

She had a dentist appointment after school on Monday. There was no way her dad would let her miss that! Then Tuesday she had another game.

Plus she would have to get someone to take her to the hobby shop so she could buy clay for her diorama. Also, she would have to go to the library to look up the facts for the index cards Mrs. Yoshida wanted.

It was an awful lot to cram into just five days.

Michelle had to do it though. She had no choice.

Chapter

9

♥ Michelle checked the clock on the living room mantel. It was after midnight on Sunday. Way after midnight.

Her diorama was due Wednesday—and she wasn't even halfway done! Plus she hadn't started working on the facts for her index cards. She was so, so sleepy. Her eyes kept closing.

But she couldn't go back to bed. Not yet. She had to get some more work done first.

Maybe I should turn on the TV, she thought. That keeps me awake.

Michelle reached for the remote. Then she set it back down.

Bad idea. The TV did keep her awake. But all she did was watch show after show.

What else can I do? she wondered.

I know! Ice!

Michelle crept into the kitchen. She took an ice cube out of the freezer and ran it over her forehead. Brrrr!

She rubbed the ice over her cheeks, and her chin, and her nose. Even her ears. Her whole face started to tingle.

Michelle grabbed another ice cube out of the freezer and dropped it down the back of her nightgown. She hopped up and down as the ice made a cold, wet trail down her back.

That woke me up! Michelle thought.

She hurried back to the living room and sat down on the couch. She opened her book on Egypt and started to read. She needed more facts for her index cards.

Hey, here's a good one, Michelle thought. If you unwrapped a mummy and sewed all the strips of linen together, it would be longer than four football fields. Awesome!

Michelle wrote that down in her notebook and kept reading. Her eyelids felt heavy. So heavy. She had to close her eyes. Just for a second.

No! She needed another way to stay awake—and fast.

I'll stand on my head, she thought. The man on *How to Do Everything Better* said that makes your brain work harder.

Michelle pushed herself into a headstand with her feet resting against the wall. But when she stood back up, she still felt sleepy—*and* dizzy.

Every night it's getting harder and harder to stay awake, Michelle thought.

The next morning Stephanie stomped into the kitchen. "I hate this," she said. "Today's school spirit day, and everybody is supposed to wear the school colors, green and yellow. But the only green thing I've got is this shirt, and it's too tight. I look like a stuffed toad." She flopped down into a chair.

Danny set a plate of waffles in front of her. "I hope you're a toad that eats walnut waffles," he said. "We're out of flies."

Stephanie made a face at him.

Michelle giggled. Then she remembered something she'd seen a model do the night before, on one of those shop-at-home shows. "Don't you have a yellow T-shirt?" she asked Stephanie.

"Yeah? So what?" Stephanie answered.

"Put the yellow T-shirt under the green shirt," Michelle explained. "Then unbutton the shirt and tie it at your waist. Roll up the sleeves too," she instructed.

Stephanie grinned. "I'll be right back." She bounced up and hurried out of the kitchen.

"I'm going to start taking you shopping with me," Danny told Michelle. "I could use my own personal fashion expert."

"I don't know, Dad," D.J. said. "Have

you noticed that the fashion expert has her shirt on inside out? And she's wearing one white sneaker and one pink one."

Michelle felt her cheeks turn red. She *was* pretty sleepy when she was getting dressed. I have to start paying more attention, she thought.

Michelle bent down to take off her shoes, and knocked over her milk. Danny rushed over with a sponge and wiped off the table.

The sponge reminded Michelle of something the man on the TV show *How to Do Everything Better* said last night.

"Hey, Dad, you should put a dry sponge in the vegetable crisper. It keeps your vegetables fresh longer."

D.J. and Danny stared at her. "How do you know that?" D.J. asked.

"Yeah," Danny added. "What's going on with you? Have you been hanging out with Heloise, or something?"

Oops. Michelle couldn't tell them she had learned all this stuff from watching TV in the middle of the night. She squirmed in her seat.

"Who's Heloise?" she asked, trying to distract them. She stood and carried her plate to the sink. "I don't know anyone named Heloise."

"She writes household hints for the newspaper," D.J. explained. "Come on, Michelle. Tell us your secret."

Michelle's cheeks burned. What could she say? She couldn't tell them the truth. "I . . . uh . . . I guess . . ." she stammered.

Danny and D.J. were watching her, waiting for an answer. "Uh . . . I . . . guess I got it from Heloise," she said quickly. "I'm really into reading the newspaper, you know? I . . . um . . . I think it's really important for kids to know what's going on in the world, don't you?"

Michelle picked up a sponge and started wiping off the counter.

"But you don't read the—" Danny began.

"Wow!" Michelle exclaimed. "It's late. I've got to go!" She jumped up and rushed out the door before D.J. or Danny could say another word.

Chapter 10

♥ "Hey, Michelle, look," Lucy yelled from across the playground. She pointed to her forehead. "I've got bangs! My mom cut them for me."

"You look great," Michelle called.

Cassie rushed over to Michelle and stopped her before she reached Lucy. "Uh, Michelle, I wanted to ask you something."

Cassie glanced around the playground. Then she leaned close to Michelle. "Do you know what will get rid of my freckles?" she whispered.

"Wait a minute," Michelle said. She gave a big yawn. "There was something . . . what was it?" She thought hard. "Oh, yeah. You put soy sauce and chopped-up onions on them. It makes them lighter."

"Are you sure?" Cassie said. "That sounds weird."

Michelle shrugged. "That's what they said on TV."

"Hi, guys!" Mandy called. She dropped her backpack in front of them and smiled. "What's up?"

"Cassie was just asking me . . ." Michelle began. Then she saw Cassie shaking her head. I guess she doesn't want anyone to know she wants to get rid of her freckles, Michelle thought. "For some . . . advice," she said.

"I need some too," Mandy answered. "Is there something that will make my hair shinier? You know, like the hair people have in shampoo commercials?"

Michelle thought for a second. "There's

something you can put in it. Um, egg yolk. It makes it shiny. Yeah, that was it. But you have to be sure to rinse it out with hot water."

"Egg yolk. Hot water. Got it. Cool," Mandy said. "Thanks."

"Michelle!" Sophia Moffet, a girl from Mrs. Yoshida's class, ran up and grabbed Michelle's arm. "Listen," she said, lowering her voice. "Do you know how to get rid of warts? I've got one on my little finger. See?" Sophia held up her hand.

"Uh . . ." Michelle blinked hard. She was so tired, her eyes burned. "Mix up some baking soda and vinegar, and rub it on every night." She hoped she was remembering it right.

"Awesome!" Sophia said. "You know so many neat tricks!"

"Yeah," Cassie agreed. "You're the best, Michelle!"

Getting up in the middle of the night isn't just good for getting homework done, Michelle thought. It's so cool having all these people ask me for advice!

So what if she was tired? It was worth it.

Michelle trotted across the playground on Tuesday morning. She had ten minutes before class started, and she had to go to the library first. She still didn't have enough facts for her index cards.

Her extra-credit project was due Wednesday. She had only one night left to put the finishing touches on her diorama and do the rest of her fact cards.

How was she going to stay up another night? She got only two hours of sleep Monday night. And just three on Sunday.

"Michelle! We have to talk to you!"

Michelle glanced over her shoulder and saw Cassie, Mandy, and Sophia hurrying toward her.

"Later, okay?" Michelle called. "I have to go to the library."

"Now!" Sophia yelled.

She sounds really angry, Michelle thought. She stopped and turned around.

"You got me in big trouble yesterday," Sophia announced when she reached Michelle.

"Me?" Michelle blinked. "What did I do?"

"You told me to mix up baking powder and vinegar. You know, for this?" Sophia pointed to the wart on her little finger. "I did. It made a huge mess! It bubbled all over the place. My mom was really mad."

"Oops," Michelle said in a small voice. "Sorry."

Sophia didn't say another word. She just turned around and walked away.

"Whoa. She was really upset," Michelle said.

"So am I," Cassie told her. "I put soy sauce and onions on my freckles last night. The way you told me to."

Uh-oh, Michelle thought.

"It made my eyes water and I sneezed all

night long. It was awful. And it stained my skin purple!" Cassie cried.

Michelle studied Cassie's face. Her skin didn't look purple. "It must have faded—" she began.

"My mom covered it with makeup," Cassie interrupted. "She called the doctor and he said it would probably wear off in about a week. Thanks a lot, Michelle."

Michelle gulped. "Oops," she said. "I must have gotten something mixed up."

"You sure did!" Mandy exclaimed.

Wait. Mandy sounded as upset as Cassie. What was going on?

"Michelle, do you know what happens when you put hot water on egg yolk?" Mandy demanded.

Michelle winced. "What?" she asked softly.

"It cooks! Right in your hair!" Mandy yelled. "And it's impossible to get out!"

Michelle stared at Mandy. Every single strand of her hair was tucked under a hat.

"What are you going to do?" Michelle asked.

"My mom's taking me to the hair salon after school," Mandy said. "Maybe *they* can get it out."

"I'm really, really sorry," Michelle told them. "I messed up," she said.

"You sure did!" Cassie glared at her.

"No kidding!" Mandy glared at her too.

I must have been half asleep when I was watching that TV show. What a disaster!

Chapter

11

♥ As soon as the last bell rang, Michelle ran to the library and checked out a book on ancient Egypt.

How am I going to stay awake tonight to finish my project? she wondered. It's only three in the afternoon, and I feel as if it's three in the morning!

I'll worry about that tonight, Michelle decided. Right now I have to worry about beating the Panthers in today's game.

Michelle hurried to the bathroom and changed into her soccer uniform. She had only ten minutes to walk over to the park where the soccer game was being held.

She couldn't stop thinking about Cassie and Mandy. She felt so bad that they were mad at her.

I have to score some points today, she thought. I can't let the Dolphins down too.

Michelle ran down the soccer field as fast as she could.

The game was almost over.

The score was 4-3. The Panthers were one point ahead.

The Dolphins had to win this game. They had to beat the Panthers.

One of the girls on the Panther team stole the ball away from Jenny and took off down the field. Michelle chased after her.

Michelle's eyes burned and itched so much, it was hard for her to see the ball flying across the field. It's because I haven't been sleeping enough, she thought. She rubbed her eyes with the sleeve of her soccer shirt and kept running.

The girl kicked the ball toward one of her teammates.

Here's my chance! Michelle raced around and blocked the ball. Then she tore down the field with the ball.

One of the Panthers darted in front of her and knocked the ball away.

You're not keeping it, Michelle thought. That ball is mine. She ran as hard as she could and circled around the girl. She stuck out her foot to trap the ball.

Michelle's foot got tangled with the other girl's. The other girl tumbled to the ground.

Michelle felt herself lose her balance, but she managed to stay on her feet. She snagged the ball and raced down the field.

Her legs felt heavy. She was so, so tired. She pushed herself to run faster.

"Michelle, Michelle, Michelle!" the girls on her team chanted.

Michelle tried to focus on the goal. It looked so blurry. *Everything* looked blurry.

She blinked. Then blinked again.

It didn't help much. Everything still appeared fuzzy. It looked as if there were five goalies in front of Michelle—not just one!

I'm so, so tired, Michelle thought. But I can make this goal. I have to!

Michelle kicked the ball as hard as she could. It sailed into—the crowd!

"Michelle, what did you do?" the coach shouted.

Chapter

12

♥ *Phweet! Phweet!* Coach Oliver blew his whistle. He signaled a time-out. The girls ran off the field and crowded around him.

Michelle slowly followed them. The girls glared at her as she joined the circle.

"What happened out there, Michelle?" Coach Oliver asked.

"I . . . I don't know," Michelle said. "I thought I was aiming at the goal. I guess I just got turned around."

All the other girls started talking at once.

"I can't believe she did that!"

"It's not fair!"

"Michelle shouldn't even be on our team. Fourth-graders shouldn't be allowed on the all-stars."

"We only have ten seconds left to play. There is no way we'll score another goal. We just lost the game!"

"Some secret weapon!"

Michelle's stomach twisted into knots. They're right, she thought. I'm like a secret weapon for the other team.

Coach Oliver blew his whistle again. "Settle down, settle down." He held up his hands. "Let's remember, girls, that everyone makes mistakes."

Everyone groaned. Michelle stared down at the ground. She couldn't stand to look at any of them. She felt like such a jerk!

Michelle sat on the edge of her bed, yawning. She wanted to crawl back under the covers and go to sleep.

Come on, Michelle. No excuses, she thought. She had to get up and work on her diorama. It was due the next day.

This is the last time, Michelle told herself. After tonight, my diorama will be done. I'll cut back on my extra practices so I can do my homework during the day. And I'll sleep all night, every night.

I won't be sleepy for my next soccer game. Then I'll prove to everyone on the team that I deserve to be an all-star!

Michelle picked up the box that held her diorama and her supplies and tiptoed downstairs.

She turned on the TV. She wouldn't be able to stay awake without it.

Michelle made a camel out of clay and placed it in the diorama next to a couple of clay people. Done! she thought. And it looks great. The cardboard pyramid turned out really good.

Now all Michelle had left to do was copy

her facts about the pyramids onto index cards. She pulled out her cards and her notebook. Then she began to write.

Her head felt so heavy. Michelle propped it up with one hand and kept writing.

You can't give up now, she told herself.

"Michelle? Michelle honey? What are you doing down here?" Danny called softly. He shook her shoulder.

Michelle lifted her head and blinked sleepily. Then her eyes snapped wide open.

Dad! He caught her downstairs! What was she going to do?

He reached over and pulled something out of her hair. He stared down at it. "It's a camel," he said finally. "You had a camel stuck in your hair."

Oh, no! I smashed the camel from my diorama, Michelle thought.

She glanced down at her diorama and

gasped. The pyramid had a big dent in one side. Three of the clay people were smashed together.

I fell asleep with my head on top of the diorama, Michelle realized. I've ruined it!

Chapter
13

♡ Tears welled up in Michelle's eyes. "I don't believe it," she said. "I messed up again."

"You want to tell me what this is all about?" Danny asked.

Michelle blinked, and two tears ran down her cheeks. "I got up in the middle of the night," she explained. "Because I had to make a diorama. I needed extra credit to get a good grade in social studies so you wouldn't make me quit the team. You know, no excuses?"

Danny's eyes widened. He ran his fingers over the dented pyramid. "You made this tonight?"

"I got up lots of nights," Michelle admitted.

"Like the night you were *sleepwalking?*" Danny asked.

"Uh-huh." Michelle bit her lip. "Are you mad?"

Danny shook his head. "Let's not worry about that right now. Why don't you tell me the whole story?"

So Michelle told him everything, starting with the night she stayed up late to do her book report.

"Wow," Danny said when she'd finished. "You've had quite a time of it, haven't you?"

Michelle sniffed. "You're not mad?"

"Well, I'm not happy about how you've handled this," Danny said. "But I think you already know it wasn't the best thing to do."

Michelle looked down. "I know," she said.

"It wasn't. I just thought I could do everything." She looked up at her father. "I'm sorry. I know I'll have to quit the team." Her chin trembled.

"Oh, Michelle," Danny said. He put an arm around her and pulled her close. Michelle buried her head in his chest.

"So what have you learned from this?" Danny asked. "Besides the fact that a diorama makes a lousy pillow?"

Michelle gave him a tiny smile. "That soy sauce and onions don't fade freckles."

Danny chuckled. "Anything else?"

"That I can't do everything. And that it's not a good idea to do homework in the middle of the night," Michelle said.

"That's a good start," Danny answered. "And how about the idea that schoolwork really has to come first? Before everything else?"

"Yes." Michelle yawned. "And that I need to sleep."

"Good," Danny said. He tried to punch out the dent in the pyramid.

"It's a total wreck." Michelle groaned.

"I don't know about that," Danny said. "We might be able to fix it."

Michelle shook her head. "It's too late."

"It's still early," Danny said, standing up. "It's not even six. And luckily, you are part of the Tanner family." Danny hurried over to the stairs. "Stephanie! D.J.! Front and center!" he yelled.

A minute later Michelle's sisters appeared at the top of the stairs, yawning and stretching. "Stephanie, you go wake up Jesse and Becky. D.J., wake up Joey. Meet back here."

"We've got a family emergency," Danny told the family when they were all gathered around him. He quickly explained Michelle's problem. "I think this diorama can be finished on time," he said finally. "If we all pitch in."

"But, Dad, we can't do her work," Stephanie said. "That's cheating."

"Agreed," Danny said. "Absolutely. It has to be Michelle's work. But I'm sure we can all find a way to make it a little easier for her. D.J., couldn't you type these notes up for her on index cards?"

"Sure, Dad, no problem," D.J. said, taking Michelle's notebook and a stack of the cards.

"Thanks, D.J.," Michelle said. Maybe this will work, she thought. Maybe I'll actually finish in time.

Stephanie looked at the pyramid Michelle held in her hand. "I've got some quick-drying glue that might work on that," she volunteered. "It's for my fake fingernails."

"Great! Thanks, Steph," Michelle cried.

"And I've got some shelf paper you could cover it with," Becky said. "It's the right color, and it just sticks on."

"I think the twins have some plastic camels, don't you, boys?" Jesse asked. "And maybe some people too?"

"Uh-huh." Alex and Nicky both nodded.

"Come on, I'll help you find them," Jesse said.

"I'll drive you to school," Joey offered.

"And I'll make breakfast," Danny added. "As usual."

Michelle grinned. She loved her big family. "Thanks everybody," she said. "I'd better get to work!"

"Congratulations," Danny said, pushing open the back door. "Your team is on the way to the playoffs!"

Cassie, Mandy, and the entire Tanner family filed into the kitchen.

"And that's not even the best part," Michelle said. She sat down at the table and took off one of her shoes. "The best part is that no one is mad at me anymore, not even you two." She grinned at Cassie and Mandy.

"Well, we couldn't stay mad forever," Mandy said. "Not at you. You're our best friend."

"We know you were only trying to help," Cassie added.

"That's good," Michelle said.

"Hey, you did really well tonight," D.J. said. "Two goals!"

Michelle grinned and pulled off her other shoe.

"I don't know what I'm going to do after your last game." Danny shook his head. "I won't be getting any exercise without those soccer drills in the backyard."

"That reminds me. I've got something for you, Dad. Come on, everybody. I want you all to see this." Michelle grabbed Danny by the hand and pulled him into the living room.

She put a tape in the VCR. "I saw this on *How to Do Everything Better,* and I taped it for you."

A muscular young man and woman appeared on the TV screen. "Now, in just fifteen minutes a day, you can get a total workout," the man said.

"Yes," the woman joined in. "This remarkable exercise program will fit into any lifestyle. Are you ready to join us?"

"See, Dad?" Michelle said. "This is just what you need. There's just one thing you have to remember."

"What's that, Michelle?" Danny smiled at her.

Michelle wagged a finger at Danny. "No excuses, Dad! No excuses!"

FULL HOUSE
Stephanie™

PHONE CALL FROM A FLAMINGO	88004-7/$3.99
THE BOY-OH-BOY NEXT DOOR	88121-3/$3.99
TWIN TROUBLES	88290-2/$3.99
HIP HOP TILL YOU DROP	88291-0/$3.99
HERE COMES THE BRAND NEW ME	89858-2/$3.99
THE SECRET'S OUT	89859-0/$3.99
DADDY'S NOT-SO-LITTLE GIRL	89860-4/$3.99
P.S. FRIENDS FOREVER	89861-2/$3.99
GETTING EVEN WITH THE FLAMINGOES	52273-6/$3.99
THE DUDE OF MY DREAMS	52274-4/$3.99
BACK-TO-SCHOOL COOL	52275-2/$3.99
PICTURE ME FAMOUS	52276-0/$3.99
TWO-FOR-ONE CHRISTMAS FUN	53546-3/$3.99
THE BIG FIX-UP MIX-UP	53547-1/$3.99
TEN WAYS TO WRECK A DATE	53548-X/$3.99
WISH UPON A VCR	53549-8/$3.99
DOUBLES OR NOTHING	56841-8/$3.99
SUGAR AND SPICE ADVICE	56842-6/$3.99
NEVER TRUST A FLAMINGO	56843-4/$3.99
THE TRUTH ABOUT BOYS	00361-5/$3.99
CRAZY ABOUT THE FUTURE	00362-3/$3.99
MY SECRET ADMIRER	00363-1/$3.99
BLUE RIBBON CHRISTMAS	00830-7/$3.99
THE STORY ON OLDER BOYS	00831-5/$3.99

FULL HOUSE™
Michelle

#5: THE GHOST IN MY CLOSET 53573-0/$3.99

#6: BALLET SURPRISE 53574-9/$3.99

#7: MAJOR LEAGUE TROUBLE 53575-7/$3.99

#8: MY FOURTH-GRADE MESS 53576-5/$3.99

#9: BUNK 3, TEDDY, AND ME 56834-5/$3.99

**#10: MY BEST FRIEND IS A MOVIE STAR!
(Super Edition) 56835-3/$3.99**

#11: THE BIG TURKEY ESCAPE 56836-1/$3.99

#12: THE SUBSTITUTE TEACHER 00364-X/$3.99

#13: CALLING ALL PLANETS 00365-8/$3.99

#14: I'VE GOT A SECRET 00366-6/$3.99

#15: HOW TO BE COOL 00833-1/$3.99

#16: THE NOT-SO-GREAT OUTDOORS 00835-8/$3.99

#17: MY HO-HO-HORRIBLE CHRISTMAS 00836-6/$3.99

**MY AWESOME HOLIDAY FRIENDSHIP BOOK
(An Activity Book) 00840-4/$3.99**

FULL HOUSE MICHELLE OMNIBUS 02181-8/$6.99

#18: MY ALMOST PERFECT PLAN 00837-4/$3.99

A MINSTREL® BOOK
Published by Pocket Books

**Simon & Schuster Mail Order Dept. BWB
200 Old Tappan Rd., Old Tappan, N.J. 07675**

Please send me the books I have checked above. I am enclosing $_____(please add $0.75 to cover the postage and handling for each order. Please add appropriate sales tax). Send check or money order--no cash or C.O.D.'s please. Allow up to six weeks for delivery. For purchase over $10.00 you may use VISA: card number, expiration date and customer signature must be included.

Name _____

Address _____

City _____ State/Zip _____

VISA Card # _____ Exp.Date _____

Signature _____

1033-25

It doesn't matter if you live around the corner...
or around the world...
If you are a fan of Mary-Kate and Ashley Olsen,
you should be a member of

MARY-KATE + ASHLEY'S FUN CLUB™

Here's what you get:
Our Funzine™
An autographed color photo
Two black & white individual photos
A full size color poster
An official **Fun Club**™ membership card
A **Fun Club**™ school folder
Two special **Fun Club**™ surprises
A holiday card
Fun Club™ collectibles catalog
Plus a **Fun Club**™ box to keep everything in

To join Mary-Kate + Ashley's Fun Club™, fill out the form
below and send it along with

U.S. Residents – $17.00
Canadian Residents – $22 U.S. Funds
International Residents – $27 U.S. Funds

MARY-KATE + ASHLEY'S FUN CLUB™
859 HOLLYWOOD WAY, SUITE 275
BURBANK, CA 91505

NAME:_____

ADDRESS:_____

_CITY:_____ STATE:_____ ZIP:_____

PHONE:(____) _____ BIRTHDATE:_____

1242